The Pittsburgh Night Before Christmas

Or

Where you at?

Under da klock, dahn Picksburgh, lookin' in Kaufmans' Windows!

By C. A. Neidig

Dedication

This poem is dedicated to my beautiful wife, Diana,

and to all of the wonderful people of Pittsburgh, wherever you may be.

Acknowledgements

Cover Designed by Katherine Neidig

Snowflake Art Designed by Sapann-Design – Freepik

Preface

I grew up in a rural farming community north of Harrisburg, PA, and in looking for colleges, discovered the "big city" of Pittsburgh. I came to Point Park College, now University, in 1973. At the time, Pittsburgh was a prime location for corporate headquarters, US Steel was king, Westinghouse was an industrial and engineering giant, and the Port of Pittsburgh was the worlds' largest inland port. Renaissance II had recently been completed, and the industrial northeast was on the verge of change.

But the world has changed, and nowhere is this more evident than the City of Pittsburgh. The smoking industrial giant, once the home of 27 major steel manufacturers, has now become rated among the top ten places to live. With blue skies, rivers teeming with fish (and Bass masters tournaments, regattas and riverside bike trails), impressive vistas, and three new sports stadiums, Pittsburgh does not fit the image of many Americans. In talking to people on my trips out of state, people still think of Pittsburgh as a dirty, industrial city.

Well, perceptions change slowly, while change seems to know no speed limit. This once blue-collar town now boasts an expanding white collar culture. The places that once held blast furnaces and extrusion mills now hold shopping malls, restaurants, a casino, and light industrial parks. This city, once dominated by smoke stacks that belched black sky's, now holds tall glass buildings reflecting the blue colors of the sky.

My wife grew up in East Liberty (S'liberty) and when her family drove to the South Hills to visit relatives, would pass several steel mills (called "still mills", hence the name, Pittsburgh Stillers). Her mother would casually and faithfully remark, "The fire from those mills will never go out." Well, after having numerous generations grow up to find their place in the mill or in service to the mill, this was the unshakeable, undeniable reality. It was the reality of generations of hard working "mill hunks" and their families.

The transformation of Pittsburgh from steel belt to rust belt to tech belt has been dramatic, and I can't help but believe that it is the heritage and strength of the people that has helped to pull them through this change, and in the tenacious clinging to ethnic traditions. There are 97 distinct ethnic neighborhoods, each with its' own culture and heritage. These are passed down through successive generations, but all with a view that they have something unique to contribute to the larger urban landscape. That they belong.

I discovered a rich Italian heritage in Pittsburgh by meeting and marrying my classmate at Point Park University, Diana. It was my first experience with cultural shock, coming from a staid German farming community. But the ride has been great, my extended Italian family has been a blessing, and this poem is an attempt to express my admiration and affection for them and for the city of Pittsburgh.

Merry Christmas, to a family and city who have my true affection!

A Pittsburgh Night Before Christmas

T'was the night before Christmas, the snow it was deep,

As I sat on the parkway and nodded asleep.

The roads were like ice, the salt crews weren't ready

And people were spinning their "tahrs" like Andretti.

The hilly-street city, all "slippy" with snow,

With cars sliding sideways and some being towed.

The cobblestone pavements, more bumpy than not,

With snow covered potholes, suspensions were shot.

The ice on the crest of the new fallen snow,

Had traffic ensnaring my car like a bow.

The radio played B.E.Taylor in season,

Which gave me a joy for the very best reason.

I stopped at the "haus" and climbed up to the stoop

(The forty-step flight seemed like eighty to boot).

I stood for a moment to take in the scene

(I love when the snow covers every dark thing).

The clattering noise on the fresh fallen snow,

Came from gutters that crackled with freezing rain flow.

The Christmas lights strung on the houses below,

Gave the chairs holding place for our parking a glow.

The wind from the rivers blew up our high street,

And froze all my fingers, my nose and my feet.

The gas meter whirred with a bright, clicking sound,

And I knew that this cold front my wallet would pound.

Then turning and jerking to open the door,

I slipped on some ice and I swore something tore.

When what to my red, bloodshot eyes should appear,

But my fat cousin, Nick, with his hand on a beer!

I looked in his eyes, and thought I saw mischief,

But laughed when I saw his eyes twinkle with Christmas.

A shake of his hand, and a nod from his head,

Soon gave me to know that I'd be in great dread.

His face was all red and his chin was all hairy,

(He was already sloshed, and that happens, not rarely)!

A new cherry pipe he held tight in his teeth,

(He had pilfered my best, so I gave him some grief).

Hey, "Kennywood's open", I said on the sly,

As he reached down to zipper, the beer can did fly!

He bellowed "git aut" in amazing reply,

And I stood for a moment to stifle my cry!

The small house was so full of family and friends,

It took me a long time to mingle and blend.

The mood was so bright and the feeling so joyous,

I swear our carols rang like a Mendelssohn chorus.

The kids were excited from socks up to head…

And I knew there'd be no way to get them to bed!

The wife was dressed up like a queen on retreat,

And she smiled Christmas joy on her rosy red cheeks.

The ornaments hung on the tree with great care,

Most of them themed with some Pittsburgh affair.

And nutcrackers lined all the mantels and shelves,

Like little toy soldiers created by elves.

The smell from the kitchen soon tickled my snout,

With seven fish dishes, pierogies and kraut.

The light from the oven soon gave me to pause,

As I pondered what cookies were baking for Claus.

I opened the oven and what did I see,

But six angel cookies, all staring at me!

When no one was looking I took a big bite,

Then screamed like a demon and looked for some ice.

When things settled down, after redding up mess,

And trying to calm down, and catching my breath,

And thinking it's time for a shot and a toast,

I reached for the Strega, and poured out the most.

And honored dear Santa, who taught us to give,

And laugh while we do it, and live and let live.

Then toast La Bafana, the poor wandering girl,

Who looks for our Savior throughout the whole world.

The girls were all busy with cooking the meal,

So me and the boys talked of "Big Bens" appeal.

Our black and gold heroes, we hope will prevail,

When playoffs are pending, our "Stillers" won't fail.

The table was set in a beautiful sight,

And I poured the wine freely, yes really, just right.

The comfort I felt from eyes shining with love…

Or was it the angel hair served from above.

The food was so good, and the faces so merry,

I couldn't help eating one last cordial cherry.

Then crashed on the couch before going to Mass,

Then raced into dress clothes and drove away fast.

The church was done-up in a wonderful sight,

And it filled us with wonder on this Christmas night.

As people poured in and were crowding the floor,

I knew there'd be no way to head for the door.

The people at Mass, some were drunk, with heads bowed,

Though I tried hard to whisper, was clearly too loud.

Babushkas were tending their grandkids with care,

Protecting with kisses and big hugs to spare.

The hearts of the people, so warm and so close,

In cold winter winds keep us comfy as toast,

The smiles to acknowledge to family and friends,

That hope is our journey and love is our end.

The ethnic groups gathered as all of our friends,

The Polish, Italians, and Germans, we blend,

And know that we're blessed to be living here still,

  Cause so many left town when they closed down the mills.

The priest in high season was leading our flock,

But he had to stay sober till church doors were locked.

He makes Christmas special, he helps pull us through,

Through good times and bad times, in history's view.

The crèche on the altar, where Jesus' head lay,

The King of Kings' throne is a manger of hay.

Saint Francis the wise man has taught us to see,

The gift of salvation, in humble degree.

The choir sang so sweet, I was carried away,

And I didn't snap out till the following day.

The presents were set and I wondered by whom,

Hey, it's Christmas, its magic, and I'm in the mood.

We opened our presents and thanked one and all,

Then packed up our gifts and our goodies to call,

And hit the snow highways, as coursers they came,

And rolled down the windows, and called them by name.

Hey you, Studda Bubba, get off the darn phone,

You Paisan, and Cumbad, or freaking Cafone?

As we shook at each other and gestured with flair,

I knew in a moment the spirit we share.

The view of our Pittsburgh from Washington peak,

With miniature trains and three rivers so deep,

Yes, Pittsburgh in winter with no salt to spare,

Will find the streets white when the slush freezes there.

We got behind somebody stuck on a hill,

And I yelled, "Move that Chivy, or you know that I will."

Then I heard him yell back, as he slid out of sight,

"Merry Christmas, yinz jagoffs, cause yinz ain't wrapped too tight!"

That's It Fort Pitt,   An'at,   Dahn 'ere!

Lexicon:

Angel Hair- Cappelini, very fine-strand spaghetti or pasta

Babushka- Russian for Grandmother (literally means scarf or head covering)

B.E. Taylor- Native Pittsburgher who writes and sings great Christmas songs.

Cafone- Italian for jagoff

Cumbad- Italian for very close friend

Jagoff- A jerk

Kennywood- One of the remaining amusement parks in Pittsburgh, but "Kennywoods Open" has always been used to inform gentlemen that their fly was open.

La Bafana- Italian "Santa Clause" or Christmas icon who gives gifts at Christmas while searching for the three wise men, who stopped at her house to ask directions, and asked her to join them on their journey to find the New Born King. But she was too busy working, so they left without her, and now she still searches for them, giving gifts as she journeys.

Paisan- Italian for countrymen

Pierogi – Polish "dumpling" with meat or potato fillings

Seven Fish Dishes- (Italian) Dried Salt cod, smelts, eel, calamari (squid), octopus, anchovies, and sardines. (depending on region, some will list different fishes)

Strega- Fine Italian Liquor (Literally means "witch")

Studda Bubba- Polish for Grandmother

About the Author:

Andy Neidig came to Pittsburgh in 1973, from Halifax, PA, to study at Point Park University and married his classmate, Diana, from East Liberty. Andy wrote a Christmas newsletter every year for comic relief, but decided to write a longer Christmas poem to show his fascination, admiration, and love for his family and the people and culture of this wonderful city. Andy is retired from the Department of Defense, and now works as an engineer for Westinghouse.

Made in the USA
Columbia, SC
11 December 2023

28245660R00019